The Day Jimmy's Boa Ate the Washing

TOPIC NUMBER ONE
CORN
NOTE: THERE WILL BE A QUIZ WHEN WE RETURN TO CLASS.
UNDERSTANDING CORN & POULTRY
CORN

The Day Jimmy's Boa Ate the Washing

by TRINKA HAKES NOBLE

pictures by STEVEN KELLOGG

HIPPO BOOKS
Scholastic Book Services
London

Scholastic Book Services Inc
10 Earlham Street, London WC2H 9LN

Scholastic Inc
730 Broadway, New York, NY 10003, USA

Scholastic Tab Publications Ltd
123 Newkirk Road, Richmond Hill,
Ontario L4C 3G5, Canada

Ashton Scholastic Pty Ltd, Box 579, Gosford,
New South Wales, Australia

Ashton Scholastic Ltd, 165 Marua Road,
Panmure, Auckland, New Zealand

First published by the Dial Press, New York.

First published in Great Britain by
Hutchinson Junior Books 1980
Reprinted 1986

Published in paperback by Scholastic Book Services Inc., 1984

Typeset in Plantin by Keyline Graphics Ltd, London NW6
Printed and bound in Hong Kong by Everbest Printing Co., Ltd.

For Sandy and Randon,
my very best friends
T.H.N.

For Melanie and Tom,
with love
S.K.

"How was your class trip to the farm?"

"Oh ... boring ... rather dull ... until the cow started crying."

“A cow … crying?”
“Yes, you see, a haystack fell on her.”

"But a haystack doesn't just fall over."

"It does if a farmer crashes into it with his tractor."
"Oh, come on, a farmer wouldn't do that."

"He would if he were too busy yelling at the pigs to get off our school bus."

"What were the pigs doing on the bus?"

"Eating our lunches."

"Why were they eating your lunches?"
"Because we threw their corn at each other,
and they didn't have anything else to eat."

"Well, that makes sense, but why were you throwing corn?"

"Because we ran out of eggs."

"Out of eggs? Why were you throwing eggs?"

"Because of the boa constrictor."
"THE BOA CONSTRICTOR!"
"Yes, Jimmy's pet boa constrictor."

"What was Jimmy's pet boa constrictor doing on the farm?"
"Oh, he brought it to meet all the farm animals,
but the chickens didn't like it."

"You mean he took it into the hen house?"

"Yes, and the chickens started squawking and flying around."

"Go on, go on. What happened?"
"Well, one hen got excited and laid an egg, and it landed on Jenny's head."
"The hen?"
"No, the egg. And it broke – yucky – all over her hair."

"What did she do?"

"She got cross because she thought Tommy threw it, so she threw one at him."

"What did Tommy do?"

"He ducked and the egg hit Marianne in the face."

“So she threw one at Jenny but she missed and hit Jimmy, who dropped his boa constrictor.”

"Oh, I know, and the next thing you knew, everyone was throwing eggs, right?"

"Right."

"And when you ran out of eggs, you threw the pigs' corn, right?"

"Right again."

"Well, what finally stopped it?"
"We heard the farmer's wife screaming."
"Why was she screaming?"

We never found out, because Mrs. Stanley made us get on the bus, and we sort of left in a hurry without the boa constrictor."

"I bet Jimmy was sad because he lost his pet boa constrictor."

"Oh, not really. We left in such a hurry that one of the pigs didn't get off the bus, so now he's got a pet pig."

"Boy, that sounds like a really exciting trip."
"I suppose so, if you're the kind of kid who likes class trips to the farm."

GRANDPRIX

OUR
BOA